FANTASY LAND FAIRY TALES

The Emperor's New Clothes

ph

Long, long ago there lived an emperor who wanted to be well-dressed. His tailors made him new clothes every single day.

A day came when his tailors could not think of any new designs. The selfish emperor yelled in anger,

''I have worn this coat before! I should never wear the same clothes twice!''

The courtiers made an announcement. It said,
"Anyone who makes the emperor a
new suit of clothes will be rewarded."
All the tailors in the land tried their best to please the
emperor, but none of the clothes suited him. The emperor
was too vain to realise that he was too plump.

One day two swindlers came to the castle.

"We have travelled all the way from Persia to please you, Your Majesty," they said. "We are weavers who make very special cloth. Our special cloth cannot be seen by anyone who is stupid."

"Hmm. That sounds interesting. I will be able to tell who is clever and who is stupid. All right. Start weaving at once," said the emperor, and he gave them a lot of money.

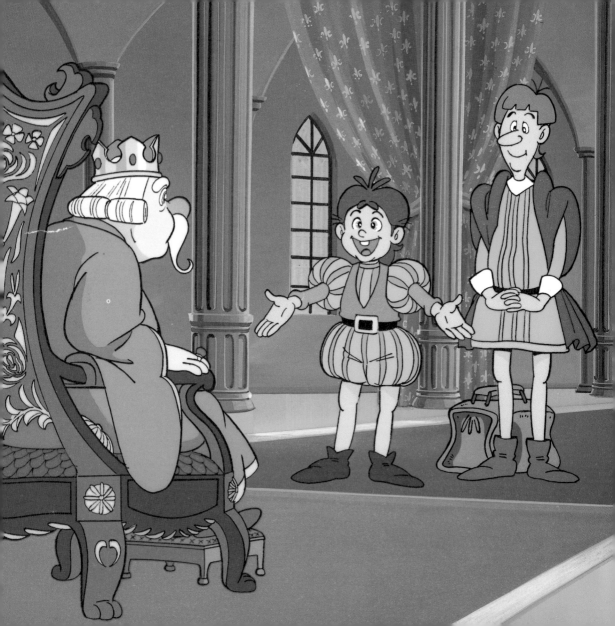

The weavers hid the money and pretended to weave a special cloth. The sound of the loom went click, clack, click, clack, till late at night.

The emperor wanted to see how they were getting on.

''I shall send my most honest minister,'' he thought.

The minister was sent to the weavers and was most shocked to see the empty loom. He tried hard to see something, but in vain.

The poor, old minister thought,

"Oh dear! But, if I tell the truth, the emperor will think I am stupid and not fit for my office."

So he said to the emperor,

"I have never seen such beautiful cloth. I am sure you will like it, Your Majesty."

The emperor was very pleased with the news and gave more money to the wicked weavers.

A few days later, the emperor wanted to see the cloth. He then thought,

"It would be embarrassing if I could not see it."

So this time he sent the captain of the guard. The emperor thought this man was the cleverest of all. But he also could see no cloth. He, too, was afraid of appearing stupid and reported to the emperor,

"It is wonderful cloth, Your Majesty."

The emperor was very pleased.

"Now I do not have to be afraid . . . I must be able to see what they saw," thought the emperor. He was sure that his men were not as clever as he. The emperor left the castle with two of his courtiers.

"We hope you will like the wonderful cloth, Your Majesty," said the two courtiers. The emperor went into the room where the weavers were working. He saw nothing on the loom.

"What is this?" he thought. "Why can't I see the cloth? Am I stupid? No, no! I am not going to say I can't see it."

So he told the weavers that he liked the cloth very much. Each courtier said to himself,

"How dreadful that I cannot see it!"

The emperor gave a lot of gold to the weavers. The wicked weavers kept working, click, clack, click, clack, and soon they said they were finished with the cloth. They pretended to cut and sew it into a new suit.

They showed it to the emperor and said,

"Please look at this suit carefully, Your Majesty. Your people will surely admire you when you appear in this."

The weavers helped the emperor to get undressed. He pretended to put the new suit on. The emperor used his imagination and said,

"Oh, this is marvellous! It is as light as a feather and yet warm as well."

Then he called his courtiers and asked,

"How do you like my new clothes?"

"What a beautiful suit and how well it fits, Your Majesty!" they replied.

By this time the people in the land were talking about the emperor's new clothes.

There came a day when a parade was to take place.

"Ahem! Only clever ones can see my new suit," said the emperor as he marched along.

People shouted,

"Indeed! The emperor's new suit is wonderful. How well it fits! Yes! Yes!"

The emperor was content when he heard the people cheering.

Then suddenly, they heard a boy's voice saying,

"Look! He has nothing on at all! Your Majesty, you'll catch a cold with nothing on!"

People on the street burst into laughter upon hearing these words.

"Oh dear! I am naked! I have been fooled! How embarrassing!" thought the emperor and took the boy to his castle.

People whispered that the poor boy would be killed by the emperor but, soon afterwards, the emperor invited the boy's parents to the castle and said,

"You have a good and honest son. He was the only one honest enough to tell me the truth."

Then he gave them many gifts. From that day forward the emperor kept his mind on ruling the land rather than worrying about clothes.

First published by Joie, Inc.
Published by Peter Haddock Ltd.,
Bridlington, England.
© Shogo Hirata
Printed in Italy.